Time Goes By

A Year at a Farm

Nicholas Harris

M Millbrook Press / Minneapolis

First American edition published in 2009 by Lerner Publishing Group, Inc.

Copyright © 2004 by Orpheus Books Ltd.

Millbrook Press
A division of Lerner Publishing Group, Inc.
241 First Avenue North
Minneapolis, MN 55401 USA

Website address: www.lernerbooks.com

Library of Congress Cataloging-in-Publication Data

Harris, Nicholas.
     A year at a farm / by Nicholas Harris.—1st American ed.
          p.   cm. — (Time goes by)
     Summary: Text and bird's-eye-view illustrations portray the many activities on a farm, from spring planting to a
summer festival and the autumn harvest. Includes related activities
     Includes index.
     ISBN 978–1–58013–553–5 (lib. bdg. : alk. paper)
     [1. Farm life—Fiction. 2. Seasons—Fiction.] I. Title.
PZ7.H24339Ye 2009
[E]–dc22   2007039036

Manufactured in the United States of America
1 2 3 4 5 6 — BP — 14 13 12 11 10 09

10-8-08

Table of Contents

THIS IS THE STORY of

a year on a farm. All the pictures have exactly the same view. But each one shows a different time of the year. Lots of things happen during this year. Can you spot them all?

Some pictures have parts of the walls taken away. This helps you see inside the farm's buildings.

You can follow all the action on the farm as the months pass. The calendar on each right-hand page tells you what month it is.

As you read, look for people that appear every month. Look out especially for the farmer, her husband, their three children, and Grandma and Grandpa. Don't miss the team of scientists and their amazing discoveries! Think about what stories these people might tell about life at the farm.

a sled?

It is winter. A thick layer of
snow covers the ground and
the roofs of the buildings. The
children are having fun in the
snow. But there's work to do too!
The farmworkers take hay to
feed the animals. Others shovel
snow off the paths. A snowplow
clears one of the lanes.

January

A heavy snow

Lambing time

Spring growth

Haymaking

A summer fair

Harvesttime

Fall arrives

Winter returns

Can you find . . .

a chicken coop?

a pig?

Spring comes to the farm. A school group is visiting to see sheep give birth to lambs. The birthing is called lambing. The cattle must stay in their barn. Not enough grass is outside for them to eat. The farmer spreads fertilizer on a field. It will help the crops grow. One of the tractors gets stuck in the mud!

March

A heavy snow

Lambing time

Spring growth

Haymaking

A summer fair

Harvesttime

Fall arrives

Winter returns

Can you find . . .

a cat?

a beehive?

a scarecrow?

Later in spring, flowers bloom on the trees. Lambs play in the fields. Ducklings swim with their parents in the pond. The farmer sprays the crops to keep pests away. Runners race through the middle of the farm. A team of archaeologists starts digging. These scientists learn about the past by digging up old objects.

April

A heavy snow

Lambing time

Spring growth

Haymaking

A summer fair

Harvesttime

Fall arrives

Winter returns

Can you find . . .

a pony?

a rabbit?

a man fishing?

The warm, sunny days of summer have arrived. It is time to shear the sheep. A special shaver is used to remove the wool from the sheep. Farmworkers cut the hay. A machine forms it into bales. The hay will feed the animals next winter. Many people have come to visit the farm. Hikers pitch their tents. The scientists have found something!

A heavy snow

Lambing time

Spring growth

Haymaking

A summer fair

Harvesttime

Fall arrives

Winter returns

June

Can you find . . .

a prize cow?

a scientist?

a tractor?

a juggler?

A summer fair is in full swing. Birds soar above the action. A judge awards prizes for the best cows. People at the fair can buy balloons and watch a juggler. A band plays for a field of dancers—including Grandpa! The scientists have uncovered an old building.

July

Can you find . . .

a grill?

a butterfly?

a frog?

an archer?

a milking machine?

Campers are setting up tents at the end of a hot summer day. A sports contest is happening in the field next to the pigs. An old plane flies overhead. The scientists finish digging for the day. But the farmer is still working. She uses a combine. It cuts the wheat and pours it into a trailer.

August

A heavy snow

Lambing time

Spring growth

Haymaking

A summer fair

Harvesttime

Fall arrives

Winter returns

Can you find . . .

an ax?

a duck?

some pumpkins?

a veterinarian?

a man
picking mushrooms?

The trees have changed color. Some people pick mushrooms. Bales of straw are stacked in the barn. Straw is made from wheat stalks. The animals will sleep on straw during the winter. The farmer plows the field to make it ready for the next crop. A TV crew films the scientists.

October

A heavy snow

Lambing time

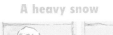

Spring growth

Haymaking

A summer fair

Harvesttime

Fall arrives

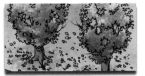

Winter returns

Can you
find . . .

a bonfire?

Grandma knitting?

a Christmas tree?

a man fixing
the roof?

a squirrel?

Winter has returned, and cold rain falls. Christmas is coming soon. The last few leaves on the trees blow away. A tractor gets stuck in the mud (again). Some of the roofs must be repaired. Only the pigs and sheep are still in the fields. Some rabbits stay snug in their burrows!

December

A heavy snow

Lambing time

Spring growth

Haymaking

A summer fair

Harvesttime

Fall arrives

Winter returns

Glossary

archaeologists: people who learn about the past by digging up and studying objects

archer: someone who shoots at a target with a bow and arrow

bales: large bundles of straw or hay that are tied tightly together

burrows: tunnels or holes in the ground where animals live

combine: a machine that harvests grain

ducklings: baby ducks

fertilizer: a substance containing chemicals that help crops grow

hay: dried grass that farm animals eat

lambing: the birth of lambs

lambs: baby sheep

shear: to cut wool off sheep

stalks: plant stems

straw: dried stems of wheat, oats, or another grain plant

veterinarian: an animal doctor

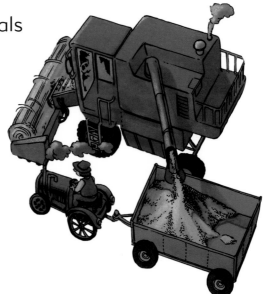

Learn More about Farms

Books

DK Publishing. *Farm Animals*. New York: DK Publishing, 2004.

Nelson, Kristin. *Farm Tractors*. Minneapolis: Lerner Publications Company, 2003.

Nelson, Robin. *From Sheep to Sweater*. Minneapolis: Lerner Publications Company, 2003.

Pelletier, Andrew Thomas. *The Toy Farmer*. New York: Dutton Children's Books, 2007.

Ross, Kathy. *Crafts for Kids Who Are Learning about Farm Animals*. Minneapolis: Millbrook Press, 2007.

Rotner, Shelley. *Senses on the Farm*. Minneapolis: Millbrook Press, 2009.

Wolfman, Judy. *Life on a Dairy Farm*. Minneapolis: Lerner Publications Company, 2004.

Websites

Farm Animal Coloring Pages—Enchanted Learning
http://www.enchantedlearning.com/coloring/farm.shtml
This Web page has outlines of many different farm animals.
Choose an animal, print out the page, and color it!

The Farm at MSI: Combine
http://www.msichicago.org/exhibit/farm/combine_inner.html
The website for Chicago's Museum of Science and Industry features an interactive diagram of a combine. Click on the names of the different parts to learn more about how they work.

Welcome to Kids' Farm—National Zoo
http://nationalzoo.si.edu/Animals/KidsFarm/
The National Zoo in Washington, D.C., has an exhibit about farm animals. Take an online tour to find out what animals are on their farm.

A Closer Look

This book has a lot to find. Did you see people who showed up again and again? Think about what these people did and saw during the year. If these people kept journals, what would they write? A journal is a book with blank pages where people write down their thoughts. Have you ever kept a journal? What did you write about?

Try making a journal for one of the characters in this book. You will need a pencil and a piece of paper. Choose your character. Give your character a name. Write the name of the month at the top of the page. Underneath, write about the character's life during that month. Pretend you are the character. What do you do all day long? Is your life hard or easy? Why? What have you noticed about the other people at the farm? Have you seen anything surprising? What? What do you hope to do next month?

Don't worry if you don't know how to spell every word. You can ask a parent or teacher for help if you need to. And be creative!

Index